This book belongs to …

Nils

Tips for Talking and Reading Together

Stories are an enjoyable and reassuring way of introducing children to new experiences.

Before you read the story:

- Talk about the title and the picture on the cover. Ask your child what they think the story might be about.
- Talk about what happens at school and why we go to school. Has your child been to nursery?

Read the story with your child. After you have read the story:

- Discuss the Talk About ideas on page 27.
- Look at the pictures on pages 28 – 29 and talk about which things Kipper and Anna did on their first day at school.
- Do the fun activity on page 30.

Have fun!

Find the coloured handprints hidden in every picture.

For more hints and tips on helping your child become a successful and enthusiastic reader look at our website www.oxfordowl.co.uk.

Starting School

Written by Roderick Hunt
and Annemarie Young
Illustrated by Alex Brychta

OXFORD
UNIVERSITY PRESS

Kipper was excited. It was his first day at school.

He was feeling a bit scared too, so he wanted to take Little Ted.

"All right," said Mum, "but don't forget your book bag."

Mum went to the classroom with Kipper. He was glad that his new friend Anna was there. A helper called Trish met them at the door.

Trish showed Kipper his peg.

It had his name above it, and his picture was underneath. Kipper put his bag on his peg.

Then Trish showed Anna and Kipper a special box. "Put your toys in here," she said. "They'll be safe."

But Kipper didn't want to put Little Ted in the box. He went back to his peg and put Ted in his bag.

9

Kipper's teacher was Miss Green. "It's time to begin,"
she said, so Mum said goodbye to Kipper.

Kipper was worried. "You will come back for me?"
he asked.

"Of course I will," said Mum. "Don't worry."

Miss Green took the register, and then they all sang a song.

Then Miss Green said, "We're going to look around the school now."

Kipper wanted Little Ted to look around the school too.

"You can show him around after school," said Miss Green.

"Here are the toilets," said Miss Green. "If you need to go, don't wait, or it may be too late."

Then Miss Green showed them the hall. Biff and Chip were doing PE.

"We have assembly in here, and lunch as well," she said.

Playtime was fun. All the children wanted to play on the logs.

"Take it in turns," said Miss Green.

Kipper wanted to get Ted, but Anna called him.
"Come and play," she said.

After play, the children did a drawing. Anna drew her lamb. Kipper drew a picture of Ted.

"Can I get Ted now?" asked Kipper.

"You can get Ted after school," said Trish. "We're going to do hand prints now."

Kipper made three green handprints. Anna made a red one.

"Can I show Ted?" asked Kipper.

"Soon," said Trish, "after school."

Anna's nose was itchy, so she rubbed her face. Now she had paint on her nose! Miss Green cleaned it off, but Anna was a bit upset.

Then Kipper and the other children made Anna laugh,
so she wasn't upset anymore.

Soon it was time to go home. "I can show my pictures to Ted now," said Kipper. He looked in his bag, but Ted wasn't there!

Kipper began to cry. "I've lost Little Ted," he said.
"Don't worry," said Trish. "We'll find him."

Just then, Anna put her hand in her bag. "Look! Here's Ted," she said. "You put him in my bag!"

Mum and Dad came to get Kipper.

"Did you have fun?" asked Dad.

"Yes," said Kipper, "but I'm going to leave Ted at home tomorrow."

Talk about the story

Where *should* Kipper have put Little Ted?

What do you think Kipper said when Anna found Little Ted?

What else do you think Kipper could do at school?

How do you feel about starting school?

At school

Talk about the things that happen at school.

Which things did Kipper and Anna do on their first day?

the register

computer

sand play

lunch time

dressing up

counting

storytime

playtime

singing a song

reading

29

A Maze

Help Kipper find Little Ted.

First Experiences with Biff, Chip & Kipper

Have you read them all yet?

Kipper's First Pet

Learning to Swim

Going to the Dentist

Going to the Doctor

Going to the Hairdresser

Fun at the Farm

Going on a Plane

Starting School

FIRST EXPERIENCES Flashcards
55 cards

Also available:
- Kipper Gets Nits!
- Going to the Hospital
- Going to the Optician
- Let's Recycle!
- Going on a Train
- Going to the Vet
- Kipper's First Match
- Kipper's First Dance Class
- A New Baby!

Read with Biff, Chip and Kipper
The UK's best-selling home reading series

Phonics

First Stories

Level 1
Getting ready to read

Level 2
Starting to read

Level 3
Becoming a reader

Level 4
Developing as a reader

Level 5
Building confidence in reading

Level 6
Reading with confidence

Phonics stories help children practise their sounds and letters, as they learn to do in school.

First Stories have been specially written to provide practice in reading everyday language.

READ WITH
Biff, Chip & Kipper

OXFORD
UNIVERSITY PRESS

Great Clarendon Street, Oxford OX2 6DP
Text © Roderick Hunt and Annemarie
Young 2007
Illustrations © Alex Brychta 2007
First published 2007
This edition published 2012

10 9 8 7
Series Editors: Kate Ruttle, Annemarie Young
British Library Cataloguing in Publication Data available
ISBN: 978-0-19-848795-1
Printed in China by Imago